Meningitis & Me

A story of the after effects of Meningitis and coping with an acquired brain injury

Nicola Jane

Copyright © 2021 by Nicola Jane

Copyright © 2024 Updated Version by Nicola Jane

All rights reserved.

No portion of this book may be reproduced in any form without written permission from the publisher or author, except as permitted by U.K. copyright law.

Contents

A Note From The Author	1
Where It All Began	3
Hospital Visit One	5
Paramedic Visit Number Two	7
Hospital Visit Number Two	8
Meningitis	10
After	13
Answers	16
Education	18
Light at the end of the tunnel?	20
Looking Forward	22
An Invisible Disability	24
Know The Signs	26
Helpful Websites	28
Social Media	29

A Note From The Author

This story was originally written as part of an anthology about Bold Characters.

I knew it was my chance to tell you about an amazing young man. The instructions I received said my story needed to be about a person in my life who's inspiring, amazing, and bold, and needed their story told. So here it is. I want to share my son's story with you because at thirteen years old, he shows enormous amounts of courage and resilience. He gets up, goes to school, and carries on, and I know he battles to keep going every single day.

His struggle is a silent one. There are no obvious signs. No limp or bruise. No way for the outside world to see how he's suffering. So, I've made it my mission in life to spread awareness about a terrible virus that's surrounded by false misconceptions and is still misdiagnosed far too often.

The virus is called meningitis. It's a virus that puts the fear of God into parents all over the world, and yet we're still not completely educated on it because although we glance at the leaflets our health advisor shoves in our hand, although we've seen the posters in the general practitioner's surgery, we still think it won't happen to us, to our children. I know this because I was one of them. I didn't know of anyone who had ever had it, and I had no clue about the real facts. If my child were ever ill, I would check for a rash that disappeared when pressed with a glass. That was the extent of my knowledge.

Where It All Began

Around three or four weeks prior to getting diagnosed, Kieran was feeling unwell with a runny nose and cough. He was always getting ill, so I wasn't too concerned—he was just one of those kids who, if an illness were doing the rounds, he'd get it. I didn't feel he was sick enough to warrant staying off school, and so each morning, I'd dose him up on Calpol (children's paracetamol) and tell him if he felt worse, to let his teacher know and she could call me.

Isn't that what all parents do? Plus, his school had a huge focus on attendance, and they were encouraging the children to attend no matter what, with the suggestion they would assess if your child were too ill for school and call you. They'd even promised daytrips to the seaside for children with good attendance. Kieran wanted that trip to Skegness so badly!

Around a week before diagnosis, Kieran became worse. He was tired and achy, and complained of headaches and flu-like symptoms. His cough was still present, and his chest was wheezy when he slept. I was starting to get concerned because there was no improvement—it seemed like he'd been ill for ages. So, we went to see the nurse at our local GP's surgery. She listened to his chest and said she couldn't hear any signs of infection, then suggested I let him rest for a few days. She said maybe it was a virus, which I feel is always the go-to answer when they don't know what's wrong.

He took a couple of days off and went back to school around midweek, even though he wasn't one hundred percent, but I felt bad being off work and so I pushed him on, thinking routine was the answer to getting him back on his feet. I remember a particular incident at school where I was called into the office because Kieran had said an inappropriate word. It was very out of character for him, and I was shocked, but the teacher also said she didn't think he was well enough to be at school and that maybe this was the problem.

So that Friday, I kept him off school again. He was feverish and tired and spent the day sleeping. He didn't really move from the sofa all day, which was unusual because often after his paracetamol, he'd be up and about. Saturday was the same.

Hospital Visit One

On Sunday morning, we awoke around seven a.m. to Kieran crying and saying he felt sick.

He vomited all over his bedroom floor and was complaining about the light hurting his eyes. I rang 1-0-1, our emergency helpline, and they sent an ambulance as a precaution.

They decided to take Kieran to hospital because his temperature was high, but overall, the paramedics didn't seem worried.

We spent a few hours in Accident and Emergency, but it was really busy and apart from monitoring him, they didn't do much. They eventually said it must be gastroenteritis, despite him having no symptoms apart from vomiting, and sent us home.

There was no improvement at all for the rest of Sunday, so I kept him in my bed, I was really concerned. Going in and out of sleep, he seemed confused and was having odd dreams. His temperature was over a hundred degrees for most of the night and I just couldn't get it down, even though I tried all the usual tricks of cold flannels on his clammy skin, the windows and doors wide open. Even stripping him down to his underpants didn't help, and then he complained how cold he was and shivered uncontrollably.

At one point, he turned to me in a sleep-like-state and said he had to leave me. I asked where he wanted to go, and he said *I couldn't go with him.*

I was terrified and spent the rest of the night watching him sleep.

Paramedic Visit Number Two

On Monday morning, Kieran woke up screaming. He was gripping the headboard of my bed and lifting himself, twisting his body like he had suddenly become possessed, and was just screaming, telling me his head hurt. I rang 1-0-1 again and the operator could hear him, so she sent an ambulance as an emergency.

A paramedic car came within ten minutes, and she ran checks. By this time, he had calmed down. She said his vitals were all fine, and if I was worried, I should take him to the local doctor when they opened, but that was still another hour away. She told me to get him up and out of bed and moving around because that would make him feel better.

She left, and I tried to get him up, but he couldn't stay awake, let alone get out of bed and support himself. He was like a dead weight.

By this time, my husband, Paul, rushed home from work. He carried Kieran downstairs, but he was still just as lifeless. In the end, he made the decision for us to go to Accident and Emergency ourselves, because he felt we couldn't wait for the GP to open. Our gut feeling was that something was very wrong.

Hospital Visit Number Two

We arrived at A&E, and while Paul had gone to park the car, I struggled to carry my lifeless child, into the hospital. Kieran's legs were stiff, it was awkward to carry him, and he cried out in pain whenever I tried to get him to walk.

I entered those hospital doors and was so relieved when the receptionist took one look and rang straight through to the emergency doctor and told him there was a seriously ill child in reception. It was all hands-on deck from there on. Kieran was rushed through to a private cubicle. They looked at his sats and said his oxygen levels were low. So, he was given an oxygen mask. He started vomiting, and they said he was severely dehydrated. He hadn't eaten or drank anything in days, so it wasn't surprising. They put him on a drip.

He started behaving oddly—one minute, he'd be crying and unsure of where he was and who we were, and the next, he was sitting up and asking if he could play on my phone. Then they told us the neurologist would be coming to take a look at Kieran. Soon after, he was moved to her ward and taken for a scan after they noticed a difference in the size of his pupils. One had grown larger than the other, and this indicated something was going on with his brain. They didn't tell us that at the time, and we were left confused and wondering what was wrong with our child. He was kept on the neurology ward for a brief time while they waited for the results, and then eventually, he was moved to intensive care. At no point did they explain there was swelling on his brain, but we have since learned this was the reason behind his move to ICU.

Meningitis

He only stayed on ICU for a day. He was acting crazy, shouting, screaming, and telling people we were trying to kill him, that he didn't know who I was. It was terrifying to see him like that. But he was disturbing other sick patients, and so, he was moved to the high dependency ward, where he had a room of his own and one nurse to every two patients. They convinced me to leave him in the care of the nurse and get some rest in one of their on-site hotel rooms. I didn't want to leave him, but he was sleeping, and they reassured me they'd call if there was any change.

That call came an hour later, and I rushed back to his room to find four doctors trying desperately to distract him from screaming for me. He clung to me so hard, that I refused to leave him again.

It wasn't until the next day that meningitis was mentioned. They decided to grow his bloods in the lab the day he'd arrived in A&E, and they were already showing signs of pneumococcal meningitis. We discovered it was because he'd been suffering from the flu for weeks before and that had developed into pneumonia. None of this had been picked up by the doctor in our local practise, despite me taking Kieran on two separate occasions.

Pneumococcal meningitis can occur when the *Streptococcus pneumonia* bacteria invade the bloodstream, cross the blood-brain barrier, and multiply within the fluid surrounding the spine and brain.

Kieran was hooked up to drips, one for his dehydration and another for medicine. He was given strong antibiotics through the line in his hand. But they kept falling out and it was painful for Kieran to have them try and get them back in each time, as his veins were shutting down and almost impossible to find. Each time they came to try and put it back in, he was pinned down by a team of staff which was so distressing for him. He'd scream and fight and use words we didn't even know he knew. I'd apologise profusely to the nurses, promising this wasn't like him. I felt almost embarrassed he was behaving so erratically, but it was because I didn't understand what was happening to him and no one explained it.

They eventually decided to put a stent in his arm. This would mean an operation, but it wouldn't fall out like the lines. This also came with issues. He wasn't allowed to eat or drink anything, and Kieran had decided that day he was hungry and was so upset when he couldn't eat. They cancelled the morning operation due to another emergency, and so the nurse came in and basically said, sod it, let's give him some cereal because they likely wouldn't operate until the following day. However, ten minutes after he'd eaten, the doctor came to see him to explain the procedure. We said he'd eaten cereal, but he didn't seem concerned. It wasn't until we got him down to the theatre that the lead doctor asked us if he'd eaten and when we said yes, she cancelled the operation again. It was eventually re-scheduled for later that evening. I'll never forget that wait whilst he was in the operating theatre. It dragged. But it went well and although he was still extremely sleepy, the moment he was awake, he interacted a little more. The antibiotics seemed to be working and with the line no longer being an issue, he was less stressed.

The only thing he struggled with was movement in his neck and walking. We had to carry him to the toilet and to shower and hold him up.

The nurses didn't seem concerned, saying it was likely due to him laying down for so long. But I felt this was over-looked, because his joints were hurting him, and it was dismissed so easily.

We were discharged from hospital a few days later which was scary, yet a relief. They said he'd recover quicker being at home and surrounded by familiar things. He couldn't walk and we hired a wheelchair to get him around, since the hospital weren't concerned about this.

We moved his mattress into our bedroom, so we were all together and I could keep a close eye on him. We also had district nurses coming in each day to continue his antibiotics.

We had to keep going back to the hospital for check-ups, but they seemed pleased with his progress, as were we.

After

I didn't notice any real changes once we were home. He was a little more emotional, but that was to be expected. He would get tired easily and his legs hurt often. But he went back to school after just four weeks from first diagnosis. Life went back to normal. Around six months later, I noticed Kieran was still frequently very tired. He was frustrated with work at school and his teacher's raised concerns.

I went to the GP, who said Kieran was at that age where boys became a little rebellious. I said I was concerned about the aftereffects of meningitis and was told that if things hadn't improved after another six months, we should take him back to see the GP.

I was counting down the days to that next appointment. Kieran had become emotional to the extreme. He couldn't keep up with schoolwork or concentrate. He was frustrated all the time and having major meltdowns at home. I was beginning to think he had ADHD because his meltdowns fit with that. We couldn't go anywhere as a family for fear of an outburst or meltdown, and he never seemed to enjoy being out in public. He would kick out at home, attacking Paul or just crying until he was so exhausted he would fall asleep. It was heart breaking to watch and we had no answers.

In the end, I changed GP practises, and the new doctor agreed that things were not good. He referred Kieran to the mental health team (CAMHs) for assessment, and Kieran's school also put in a referral to support the doctor.

The mental health team assessed Kieran around three months later and gave us things to try at home. They weren't overly concerned and thought it was just behavioural. But then Kieran began hurting himself out of frustration. He'd bang his head against the wall and scratch himself. He'd shut down and become unresponsive, and that would be followed by a breakdown of tears and anger that could last hours.

He then started threatening to kill himself, often saying he just wanted to die. In class he'd tried to cut his arm with scissors. It was the final straw, and I demanded we be referred for an emergency meeting with CAMHs.

They did another assessment and agreed to do sessions in school with him. There were six sessions in which a worker came out to school and did some emotional therapy with him to help him understand his feelings. It helped slightly. But six sessions didn't really scratch the surface and Kieran continued to need one on one time with the school's learning mentor.

It was frustrating. I remember being asked by the mental health worker what I wanted to gain from her sessions with my child. I wanted to cry at her lack of understanding because I just wanted my child to want to live. I couldn't stand to watch his suffering anymore. And, if she couldn't help him, then I needed tactics and ways in which she thought I could help him. I told her all this and she responded with some leaflets on keeping sharp objects out of his reach and locking windows so he couldn't jump from them.

One particular day, I was called to Kieran's school because he was acting odd. I ended up sitting in the sensory room with him as he went into a trance-like state, and when he eventually came around, he didn't know where he was. It scared me because it reminded me of how he behaved when he had meningitis, so I took him to the hospital. He was sent home after a few hours of being monitored, but they referred Kieran back to the original consultant who looked after him when he was first in hospital. He referred Kieran for an EEG. When that came back as normal, they tried a different EEG and then a sleep-deprived EEG. Those tests were all normal apart from signs of slowing but not enough for them to be concerned. These appointments spanned over years. Just getting a referral means then waiting on an appointment, and then, in some cases, there were assessments before the actual appointment. It was a long, drawn-out process while Kieran continued to suffer.

Answers

I began to research myself. I joined meningitis support groups on social media. It was there that someone mentioned brain injury. So, I researched that too. It fit with everything Kieran had been going through. I emailed the consultant and asked if this could be the issue, and he went away to look at Kieran's last brain scans. They showed damage to the frontal and temporal lobes. It explained so much and it was a huge relief. It meant I could continue my own research and understand it all, for once I felt like I could help him because I understood.

The consultant referred us to a specialist in brain injury, and she passed us to the BRILL Team at Queen's Medical Centre, who specialised in child brain injury.

The BRILL Team sent a wonderful woman from the Brain Injury Trust, who came to our house and spoke with us both to tell us about brain injury, and she told us which part of Kieran's brain had been affected. She understood everything we said and all the complaints, even down to Kieran's aching legs, which doctors had dismissed.

The Brain Injury Trust has been a beacon of light in a very bleak time for us and suddenly, things became clear. Having a diagnosis which meant I could understand Kieran better and I realised his behaviour was out of his control. His shutdowns were because his brain was in sensory overload and would shut him down to block it all out.

Kieran had an assessment with a neurologist who listed so many things Kieran was struggling with, things we didn't even realise. She did lots of brain tests, and we were shocked by the results. She said Kieran was struggling badly with fatigue and it was the worst case she'd seen in a long time. That was contributing to the way he was feeling and had brought on a serious bout of depression.

Kieran is unable to learn the same way as other kids in class, and so things had to be broken down and explained a little at a time. He has a terrible memory, especially when it comes to things he isn't interested in. She told us that he'd always struggle with his memory and the way his brain receives and transmits messages will always be different than a healthy person. Basically, he won't ever recover. But we won't fully understand which changes are here to stay until his brain is fully developed at around twenty-five years old.

Education

Kieran's education has suffered badly because of his needs. Any parents with a special educational needs child, will tell you that the education system is not designed for neuro-diverse children.

We were lucky in the first two years of secondary school as it was the same time Covid-19 hit. Schools were shut down and most of his learning was done at home. But by year nine, schools were back in full swing, and Kieran struggled with this, as did many children generally. To go from short hours with rest breaks, to full time education, especially when you have fatigue and other health issues, was hard.

Kieran struggled to understand the work and his teachers struggled to teach him in the way he needed. I tried hard to collaborate with the school in getting them to understand his needs. He became stressed, which in turn made his fatigue spike. He took more days off sick and began getting migraines that would mean days spent in bed.

When it came to year ten, I was a little more ready for a fight. We came to a new arrangement that meant Kieran would attend morning lessons. I dropped my hours at work, and we were both home by one o' clock. It meant afternoons he could rest. However, this soon became an issue as some of his afternoon lessons that he missed, continued onto the morning lessons he was attending, so he'd miss chunks of work and was left with no idea what was going on. Fatigue made it hard for him to catch up on work missed, and cramming so much work in became counter-productive.

Towards the end of year ten, we agreed that Kieran would drop some lessons. He would study the core subjects, Math, English and Science. It meant less GCSEs, but we hoped it would be easier on his brain and that he'd have the capacity to focus on those important subjects.

By year eleven, he was only attending those lessons. In between he'd either come home or sit in the zone which was a special unit for children with learning difficulties.

It meant I had to give up my job so I could be around for Kieran. He was home at all different times of the day and wasn't able to be left alone.

He was given extra time for exams and a time-out card if he needed breaks. He didn't exercise any of these as he hates to be different. For a teenage boy, it's important to be seen as normal as everyone around them, which only made the struggle harder.

Kieran didn't earn a pass grade in Maths or English. He was very close. But we were so proud that he'd even taken his GCSE's because there were times, we never thought that would be possible.

Due to new government laws, all children have to pass Maths and English, or they have to retake the exams until they turn eighteen. Unfortunately, there is no consideration for children with brain injuries, or any type of neuro diversity. For Kieran to retain and recall information, it's hard work. And forcing him to keep retaking, with the possibility not achieving the results he needs, is demoralising and cruel. Almost like a punishment for having a brain injury.

Light at the end of the tunnel?

Kieran is now sixteen.

Leaving school was a relief for him and us. It was the hardest time that seemed never ending. The constant battles and phone calls have left me with anxiety, and I'm sure Kieran has some scars too. He refused to go to his prom, mainly because he never wants to set foot in that school ever again.

But, towards the end of year eleven, he decided that he'd like to learn a trade and he chose carpentry and joinery.

We enrolled him in a local college and although he needed a pass in maths to get on the course, they were happy to enrol him as long as he agreed to retake maths, which was a requirement by law anyway.

We worried about all the things parents usually worry about. Would he be able to get the bus alone? Would he make friends easily? Would he be able to keep up with the work?

We showed Kieran the journey to and from college. I got the bus with him before the start date so he could get used to it. Paul drove the route and walked from the bus stop with him. And that first week was stressful as parents. We worried continually. But he did it. He got the bus with no problems.

It's only been a term at college, but so far, he seems to be doing well. He loves his course and says he can keep up with he work. The fact there's a lot of practical helps. He isn't enjoying English or Maths, because he still doesn't understand it. But the fact he's attending it and trying, is all we can ask. The likely hood is, he may never pass, but we have talked about getting a one-on-one tutor to help. It's a fine line because if we overload him, fatigue will take over. College won't allow him to work from home for these lessons, and insist he attends them in college, even though he doesn't benefit from them.

Kieran has dreams for his future. He wants to complete the first two years of his course and then find an apprenticeship. He plans to become a self-employed carpenter one day. And with his determination, I have every faith he will achieve that.

Looking Forward

We're lucky. Meningitis didn't take his life. But it still stripped us of the son we once knew. It took away his ability to function like other boys his own age. It brought us much closer as a family, but also changed the dynamics. Our eldest son, Owen, lost out on a relationship with Kieran. The years they should have been playing together, teasing each other, and doing what normal brothers do, were surrounded with trauma.

Kieran is hard to read. He doesn't show any emotion, and the only way I know anything is wrong, is when he goes quiet. He doesn't particularly like touch. He struggles to read situations and people. His brain doesn't always keep up when he's interacting, and he forgets words as he's speaking. He doesn't retain information and learns better through practical work. He struggles with things that take many steps to complete, i.e. cooking.

But he is funny and can make us all laugh. It's hard to ever be mad with him because he's got this cheeky Chappy thing going on and can win us around easily. He's determined and wants to be successful in life. He loves his dogs, sometimes more than humans! He sees things very black and white, and he can make a complication seem so easy to solve. Most importantly, he's happy. Finally, he's happy. And that's all I ever wanted.

For anyone living with meningitis, I would say, it's hard, but you're not alone. Reach out to charities such as the Meningitis Trust, the Brain Injury Trust, and also Meningitis Now. Look for the groups on Facebook and speak to people who are going through it. There will be someone who gets it when the rest of the world thinks you're going mad. And hang in there.

As always with meningitis, I say, trust your instincts, no matter if you're a parent or it's affecting someone close to you. I should have trusted my instincts when so many professionals turned me away.

I was right—Kieran was seriously ill all those years ago, and I was also right when I told them my son was not mentally ill, but struggling with the after-effects of the illness.

It has been a nine-year battle, but it feels like it's getting easier as time goes on. I'm sure we'll encounter issues and problems as he grows, but we're more hopeful about his future now.

An Invisible Disability

I think the hardest part of all is he's been left with an invisible disability, and we are constantly having to explain it to people, even family. When meningitis takes limbs, people can see it and can sympathise. There's no way a school would tell a person to run in P.E. if they've lost their legs. But with an invisible disability, you're constantly being challenged and questioned. How can I prove that he's suffering from fatigue or that he doesn't remember the work he did yesterday? He isn't faking it, but you're made to feel like a liar most of the time, or that you're making excuses for him. It's a never-ending battle. Kieran is the bravest, strongest child I know. He keeps going when the world doubts him. He fights even when he's too tired to. And yes, sometimes he wants to give up, but we encourage him to battle on. He tries to be the best version of himself, and one day, he'll take ownership of his brain injury and be able to fight his own battles. But until that day, I'm happy to be his voice.

We should never judge what we don't understand, and we should always try to show understanding of invisible disabilities.

I'll go on spreading meningitis awareness because it's so important to me to prevent another family from suffering like we have. Spot the signs early and get treatment to reduce the aftereffects. Remember not to wait for a rash—it doesn't always appear!

Know The Signs

The symptoms of pneumococcal meningitis usually come on rapidly. An infected person may develop the following:

- Chest pain
- Chills
- Confusion
- A cough
- A headache
- A high fever
- Vomiting
- Weakness

Other possible symptoms with this form of meningitis include:

- Agitation
- Irritability
- Rapid breathing

- Stiff neck

- In infants, the soft spot on the head, which is called the fontanel, may bulge outward.

Thank you for reading Kieran's story. If this helps just one more person, I've achieved what I set out to do.

Helpful Websites

Meningitis Now
Child Brain Injury Trust
The Children's Trust
Meningitis Research Foundation
Meningitis Trust

Social Media

Since leaving my full-time job, I have taken up writing full time. I write romance and I'm self-published. I'm proud of everything I have achieved, and the fact I get to work my hours around caring for Kieran is a bonus. You'll find me here . . .

My Facebook Page

My Facebook Readers Group

Bookbub

Instagram

Goodreads

Amazon